A Rex Graves Mini-Mystery

SAY MURDER

~ WITH ~

FLOWERS

C. S. CHALLINOR

Second Edition 2017

Cover art [Anke] © Can Stock Photo, Inc., 2015

Book cover, design, and production by Perfect Pages Literary Management, Inc.

ISBN-13: 978-1726179645
ISBN-10: 1726179648

Praise for the Rex Graves Mystery Series:

Christmas Is Murder (*starred review*)
"The first installment in this new mystery series is a winner... A must for cozy fans." ~*Booklist*

"Challinor will keep most readers guessing as she cleverly spreads suspicion and clues that point in one direction, then another." ~*Alfred Hitchcock Mystery Magazine*

Murder at Midnight
"What could be better for Agatha Christie whodunit fans than an old-fashioned, Scottish country house murder on New Year's Eve?" ~*Mystery Scene*

"This is a classic country-house mystery, with modern day twists and turns adding to the fun." ~*Booklist*

Murder Comes Calling
"Smooth prose will keep cozy fans turning the pages." ~*Publishers Weekly*

"This seventh in the series nicely mixes procedural detail and village charm and will appeal to fans of Deborah Crombie and Anne Cleeland." ~*Booklist*

Judgment of Murder
"Intriguing... Readers will eagerly await Rex's further adventures." ~*Publishers Weekly*

Upstaged by Murder
"...fans—and there are many—will be shouting, 'Bravo!'" ~*Booklist*

THE REX GRAVES MYSTERY SERIES

Published by Midnight Ink:

Christmas Is Murder
Murder in the Raw
Phi Beta Murder
Murder on the Moor
Murder of the Bride
Murder at Midnight
Murder Comes Calling
Judgment of Murder
Upstaged by Murder

Published by Perfect Pages Literary Mgmt, Inc.:

Murder at the Dolphin Inn
Prelude to Murder
SAY MURDER WITH FLOWERS: A Rex Graves Mini-Mystery
SAY GOODBYE TO ARCHIE: A Rex Graves Mini-Mystery

SAY MURDER WITH FLOWERS

~ * ~

REX GRAVES stood by in a dark grey suit, watching the proceedings. The mourners would in all likelihood take the bulky, bearded redhead to be an usher or an assistant to the funeral home's director, which suited his purpose for now.

First in line went the parents, shrunk in grief, Sir William Howes extending a comforting arm around his wife's fragile shoulders. The viewing casket, nestled among the floral arrangements and formal wreaths, enveloped the body of Elise Howes, struck down in the bloom of youth as she carried home a bunch of yellow chrysanthemums, subsequently found strewn across New Bond Street. Muted sobs punctuated the chilled silence as the small gathering passed in single file before the coffin lined with cream satin. The women in black veils, the men sombrely attired, contrasted with the white lilies, gerberas and roses.

The deceased's father, adamant Elise's death had been no accident and entertaining a suspicion of murder, had given his solicitor *carte blanche* to retain the services of a private investigator. In view of Rex's success in solving murder mysteries, Mr. Whitmore had prevailed upon the Scottish barrister to solve this most distressing of cases. The hit-and-run driver had not been found. CCTV cameras had failed to record the incident, and no eye witnesses had come forward, except for a man exiting a nightclub in a neighbouring street. He had heard a car rev up—a sports car, judging by the throaty pitch of the engine—followed by a thud, a whining protest of acceleration and, finally, a squeal of tires as the vehicle careened around the corner, with only the taillights visible as the reveller reached the scene. The young woman had been dragged a few feet beneath the vehicle and abandoned on the road.

According to the eye witness, the victim's last gasping words before losing consciousness had been "Chris" and "Jean," or maybe "Jen." She had died in the ambulance. A passer-by had noticed a grey van among the cars parked on the street where the accident occurred. And now Sir William Howes, a cabinet minister described in political circles as ruthless and intractable, was most anxious to bring the culprit to justice, whomever it was.

Rex had agreed to adjust his schedule in Edinburgh and taken the train from Waverley Station to London. He had met briefly with Sir Howes at his Belgravia home before reaching the funeral parlour in time to take his first glimpse of the deceased's nearest and dearest, previously described to him in detail by the meticulous Mr. Whitmore.

~ * ~

Passing presently under Rex's review as she paid her respects was Elise's business partner, a luscious brunette, most becoming in her mourning suit. Eyes obscured by a gauzy veil covering half her face, full lips trembling with emotion, she placed a rosebud in the casket. Shannon Smythe was not quite the femme fatale Whitmore had suggested, perhaps. Still, who could resist such a woman? An old fogey like himself, for starters, Rex reasoned. But where there was a beautiful woman there was usually drama.

And drama in its ultimate manifestation—murder—was his hobby, as well as forming a large part of his prosecutorial work at the High Court of Justiciary in Scotland's capital.

Upon first hearing the shortlist of suspects, he thought the cabinet minister might be jumping to conclusions, his mind unhinged by sorrow at the untimely death of his daughter. The family solicitor had gone on to explain that the Howes girl was wealthy in her own right. Her business venture, *Head Start!*, had taken off since Will and Kate's Royal Wedding, when the creative array of hats and "fascinators," such as those worn by the daughters of the Duchess of York, had caught the public's attention. The Queen's Diamond Jubilee had only served to reinforce the craze, as would, no doubt, the christening of the new prince.

Elise and her founding partner, Shannon Smythe, a friend from the London School of

Design, had capitalized on the national historic events and signed lucrative deals with higher-end department stores to supply head gear riffed off top designers. Not a coincidence, Rex's legal colleague had emphasized, that Elise should be "got rid of" to benefit Shannon, especially since the partner's alibi had proved to be pure fiction. The girl might well have something to hide, said Mr. Whitmore, speaking on behalf of Sir Howes.

Sir Howes' reasons for suspecting Ms. Smythe stemmed from her flimsy alibi for Friday night, subsequently disproved by the police; and the fact she drove a silver Fiat 500. The gold-plated buckle on Elise's shoulder bag, recovered intact at the scene, had been scraped and flecked with silver paint. Yet only a few minor dents and scratches had been found on Ms. Smythe's front bumper, and there was no evidence of a touch-up. That she had lied to police about the film she'd seen at the West End cinema was more revealing. She had given a synopsis of the plot, only to be informed that the movie was not yet showing in the UK, and she must have based her recollections on the preview. She had responded, with a shrug, that she'd stayed home painting her toe nails, listening to Adele on her iPod, and had from then on refused to budge from her story.

Rex was intrigued by her reaction to being outed, as relayed by the solicitor. After all, a shrug denoted something less urgent to hide than a hit-and-run. He was determined to find out more than the police had unearthed. His sympathetic approach and Lowland Scots burr invariably produced a tongue-loosening effect on people, particularly women, and in his usual garb of tweed jacket and corduroys, he cut a far less imposing figure than in the black gown and stiff wig he wore for court.

Regarding who had given Elise Howes the chrysanthemums, the solicitor was uncertain. Elise, working late at her office that Friday night, was presumed to be meeting her fiancé at *Presto's* on Market Street, but had, apparently, been stood up. This accounted for her walking home alone late at night. The fiancé, Gino Giannelli, had denied they'd had a date, even though they frequently met at the bistro for dinner and she often stayed at his flat on weekends. The Italian was Suspect Number Two on Sir Howes' list. He might have been Number One had his daughter already been married to him, citing Elise's family fortune as motive.

The Howes' eldest daughter stood next to her parents receiving the guests. Mr. Whitmore had confided that Jennifer's life goal while awaiting her great aunts' demise—presumably the two desiccated old ladies sitting nearby dressed head to toe in black brocade—was to snag a rich husband and, to this end, she frequented high society sporting events, including Ascot, Wimbledon, and Polo in the Park. A horsey girl, her scarlet mouth showed pinched and stark in a face almost as ghostly pale as her dead sister's. The Howes gene pool had conspired to bestow the worst features of each parent on her person. Unlike her ethereally pretty sibling, Jennifer had inherited her father's prominent nose and long chin, and her mother's toneless blond hair, weighed down in both cases by black cloche hats in crushed velvet.

Rex did not fail to notice that in unguarded moments she eyed, with primal hunger, a designer-stubbled man with mussed up black hair held in place with slick gel, who could be none other than Elise's grieving lover. And Sir Howes' second prime suspect.

"Look into him as well as the girl," the minister had instructed Rex in his gleaming wood library that day.

The machismo Gino Giannelli hung back in a palm-potted corner of the funeral parlour, in conversation with one of Sir Howes' aged aunts, his dark eyes bright with tears as he performed operatic gestures of despair. During his brief visit to Sir Howes' home, Rex had gathered that the Minister of Transport did not altogether approve of the "Italian stud" to begin with, although, given his daughter's track record of broken engagements, he had not been unduly concerned about a finish line at the altar.

Giannelli's work involved the import of luxury Italian cars. "I introduced him to some rich and influential acquaintance who might be in the market for an overpriced pile of foreign metal," Sir William Howes had told Rex, handing him a snifter of brandy from a cut-glass decanter. "He even tried to sell *me* one of his fancy cars. Fat chance. I don't drive these days—I like my drink too much. Darling Elise was no good at controlling her alcohol intake either, or her reaction to it."

Indeed, Rex had learnt from his reliable source, Mr. Whitmore, that the coroner had found her alcohol consumption to be considerably elevated.

"So much safer to use a car service, I thought. Just goes to show," Sir Howes had maundered. "You try to pre-empt disaster, and it happens anyway."

The irony of the Minister of Transport using a private car service had not been lost on Rex, especially since there was no shortage of tube stations in Central London. But Sir Howes was careful enough about his image not to have a personal full-time chauffeur.

His driver of preference from Sloane Car Service was one Erik Christiansen, who now passed impassively by the coffin, black cap in his hands. Tall, with ice-blue eyes, white-blond hair and chiselled features, he was a foil to the muscular Gino Giannelli. He had been in a limo the night in question, waiting to pick up Sir Howes and his wife from a dinner party held in honour of the Italian Ambassador, bachelor-about-town Vittorio Scalfaro, an event that took place at a private club in the vicinity of the accident.

The silver stretch limo in service that night had been found to be in immaculate condition, per the police report provided by Mr. Whitmore. In any case, Sir Howes had come to trust the Danish driver implicitly, and sometimes utilized his services for delivery of time-sensitive documents and other important business.

Gino Giannelli drove a black Lancia, Whitmore had divulged. And the victim's sister, who apparently felt most comfortable on a horse, availed herself of the car service. It seemed both Howes girls eschewed public transport entirely. Rex tried not to hold their snobbishness against them. Elise was dead, and he'd accepted the task of bringing the responsible party, whether a reckless driver or a callous murderer, to justice.

~ * ~

With the sum of these facts and the faces fresh in his mind, Rex took a cab that afternoon to the bistro where Elise Howes was last seen alive. According to staff at Presto's, she had sat alone at the bar sipping chilled limoncellos, alternately checking her phone and anxiously looking around the restaurant. Finally, at around eleven o' clock, she rose from her stool after petulantly paying her tab. Tripping in her high heels on her way out, she grabbed onto a tapestry wall hanging and brought it down on herself, as witnessed by the bartender and a waiter, who rushed to her assistance. They had not thought to send her home in a taxi. A regular, she was generally in the company of Signor Giannelli. No one had thought to call him either. She had simply left, unsteady on her feet, after insisting she'd be fine and pressing another large tip in the hand of the bartender for any damage to the wall and decorative hanging.

When questioned further, no one at Presto's had seen her with the yellow flowers found at the accident, which suggested she had acquired them between leaving the bistro and getting hit by the car, an hour-long interval no one could account for.

Chrysanthemums were an odd choice of flower for a courting man, Rex reflected as he waited under the awning for a lull in the rain; especially for a man like Gino. Rex idly watched the waves of multicolour umbrellas on either side of the street, remembering when he had given an ex-girlfriend a bunch of mums in hospital. She had clearly been disappointed, informing him later, when sufficiently healed emotionally from her suicide attempt, that chrysanthemums symbolized death in certain countries in Europe.

No good deed ever went unpunished, he ruminated. Especially with women. They never told you what they really wanted, and then acted as though you should have been able to read their minds. How was he supposed to understand every nuance and significance behind flowers, whose primary purpose, he'd always thought, were to look nice, smell sweet, and cheer people up?

Had Elise Howes displayed a similar reaction to the flowers? Whom she had met or visited after she left Presto's, if not Gino, remained a mystery following Rex's informal interviews with the staff. Could a woman have given her the chrysanthemums? It wasn't her birthday, he knew from her date of birth listed in his file. Dick Whitmore, who had been in touch with the detectives on the case, had reported a two-minute call on her retrieved mobile phone from her sister Jennifer earlier that fateful evening, and a text message from Shannon Smythe entreating her partner to check out a line of hats featured in the latest edition of *Vogue*. Rex would have liked to talk to the mother, but Lady Howes had taken to her bed after the vigil and was not receiving company. Diana Howes was, as Whitmore described her, "a woman of extremely delicate nerves."

Hailing a cab on the street, Rex gave the driver the address of Elise's flat in Mayfair Mews, and asked if he knew of any flower shops in the area.

"Up 'ere," the cabbie informed him, pointing

14

to a narrow turning as they took off over the wet cobblestones. "Say It with Flowers is the name of it. But it's a one-way street and it'll take us out of our way."

Say It With Flowers, Rex knew from his mother's television viewing, was a nineteen thirties musical about an ailing London flower seller whose fellow stall owners organize a benefit at a local pub to fund her trip to the seaside.

"Is it the only florist near here?" he asked the driver.

"Only one I know of."

"Can you not find a parking space?"

"Chance'd be a fine thing."

Rex asked the cabbie to double back and take him to the shop, regardless. This proved no easy feat in the maze of streets, but finally the manoeuvre was accomplished, and Rex asked him to wait outside while he made enquiries as to who might have purchased yellow chrysanthemums on Friday night. The sales clerk, dressed in a dark green canvas apron, remembered a "dishy foreign bloke what paid cash."

"Stocky build? Dark hair?"

"And with dreamy dark eyes. Drop-dead gorgeous, he was."

Had Elise dropped dead at this charmer's hands? Rex wondered. "What time was this?" he asked.

"We was just closing. Must've been almost

midnight. We stay open late Fridays and Saturdays for the theatre crowd."

Rex thanked the young woman and left the shop. Had she gone to Gino's flat to confront him about his standing her up, if such was the case? Had he tried to mollify her with flowers as he walked her back home?

"Wot, no flowers?" The cabbie seemed disappointed when Rex returned empty-handed.

Parked off the curb, the glistening black cab impeded the flow of traffic, and irate drivers tooted their horns as they navigated around it in the downpour.

"What sort of flowers would you give your fiancée?" Rex asked the man, a fortyish skinhead possessed of a heavy jaw and thick neck.

"Roses, mate."

"Not chrysanthemums?"

The cabby glanced pityingly at him through the sliding partition. " 'Ardly. Them's granny flowers, them is. Where to now, guv? On to Mayfair Mews?"

Rex reconsidered. The rain was coming down hard, and it had been a long day. He gave the driver the address of Wellington House where he was staying.

Dick Whitmore's daughter was an investment banker currently working in Shanghai, and her London apartment was between sub-lets. A cosy studio with a small but well-appointed kitchen, it overlooked a park enclosed by iron railings containing a profusion of horse chestnut trees in full bloom. Rex was ready for the meal prepared and personally delivered by Whitmore's housekeeper, who had already stocked the refrigerator and cupboards with the basic commodities: Milk, tea, bread, biscuits, and jam. He did not plan on wasting time dining in restaurants when he could eat in peace while working on the case. He was due back in court on Monday.

~ * ~

The next morning, Rex caught up with Giannelli as he was passing through the cemetery gates after the burial service. He explained he was conducting an inquiry at the behest of Mr. Whitmore, the Howes family solicitor, and begged the fiancé's indulgence at encroaching upon his fresh grief. In point of fact, Gino did not appear overly distressed; more in a hurry to be off. Time was of the essence, Rex explained, since Sir Howes was anxious to locate the driver of the silver car in the absence of any progress made by the Metropolitan Police.

"Perhaps you were escorting Elise home on foot from Presto's and stopped on the way to purchase flowers?" Rex prompted. "In that case, it lets you off suspicion of being behind the wheel."

"I didn't see her," the Italian said with a slight accent, checking his Movedo watch. "And I didn't buy flowers."

Was it possible a handsome foreigner other than Gino had purchased chrysanthemums at Say It with Flowers that same night? On what pretext could he drag Elise's fiancé to the florist for identification by the sales clerk?

"Important engagement?" Rex asked, nodding at the timepiece on the man's darkly matted wrist.

He shrugged in an eloquent manner and gazed at Rex with defiant black eyes. His heavily hooded lids could have given him a sleepy look were he not so tense.

"When did you last see her alive, Mr. Giannelli?"

The Italian sighed. "I told the police all this. Last Sunday night. She went on a business trip the next day."

"No plans for the following weekend?"

"She was supposed to call me, and never did."

"Doesn't sound like you two were that lovey-dovey." Rex fiddled with the stem of the pipe in his jacket pocket. He'd given up smoking, but still found satisfaction in the familiar smooth feel of the stem and rosewood bowl.

"The wedding was putting a strain on us. She wanted to set a date and I wanted to wait."

"Why was that?"

Again the shrug. "Her father doesn't like me. It made things uncomfortable."

"When did you first hear about the accident?"

the Scotsman asked.

"Saturday morning. The phone woke me. It was Diana—Lady Howes—in hysterics. Her husband came on the line and said the police would be questioning everyone closely associated with Elise. It sounded like an accusation, which I did not appreciate very much."

Rex could not see any legitimate reason to delay Giannelli further at this point and did not want to overdo his unwelcome. Perhaps more could be gleaned from the alluring and smartly hatted Shannon Smythe, who had peeled away from a group of mourners at the new gravesite slotted in the wet grass.

"Miss Smythe, my name is Rex Graves, QC," he said as he approached on the path and held out his hand.

"I know who you are," she said taking it. "I saw you yesterday at the funeral parlour." Emerald eyes, green as the grass and accentuated by a glossy black brim, appraised him with frank interest. "Mr. Whitmore said you had questions about Elise's whereabouts on Friday night." Her voice was fashionable young London, imbued with an appealing huskiness.

"Aye, and I hope you'll be kind enough to answer them. Did you know of any plans Elise might have had? I realize you've already gone through all this with the police, but there's a gap in the timeline."

"I have no idea what her plans were. She was

working late Friday catching up after her trip to Paris. Her door was closed. I left the office around six. We didn't typically see each other at weekends, except professionally."

"Why was that?" Drops of rain began to fall, and Rex opened his brolly in an attempt to shield the young woman in her black silk suit and hat.

"We had our own sets of friends.

"But you were chummy in college."

"True. But then Elise started seeing Gino, and I really don't care for him and his playboy crowd. It was obvious he was using her for her money."

"In what way?"

"Only last week he hit her up for a large loan for his car import business."

"Her own private money?"

"Yes, but capital that could have been invested in Head Start! to develop our line in handbags and other accessories. Naturally, I was opposed, but Jennifer told her sister the loan was a sound investment, and Elise listened. Jenn only said that to butter Gino up, who it's obvious she has the hots for."

"I take it you dislike Jennifer?" Rex inferred from her disdainful tone.

"She likes to snoop and cause trouble."

"Give me a for instance."

Standing close to him under the brolly, Shannon Smythe gazed up at him with a gleam of amusement in her fine eyes. "You are very persistent, Mr. Graves. Well, all right then. When I stayed at the Howes' home one time when Elise and I were students, Jenn caught us sneaking out late to go to a club. She told Sir Howes, who's a strict old bugger, as you probably know. Jenn has always been jealous of her sister having loads more boyfriends. And she was positively green over Gino."

"I thought Jennifer was looking for a rich husband," Rex asked disingenuously, aware of the looks of longing Jennifer had cast in Giannelli's direction at the funeral home.

"Gino's doing all right for himself. He was expanding his business. Hence the loan."

"I hear your business was on the up and up too."

"Elise and I made a good team. I took care of the merchandising, she had the flair and the contacts. My own family is not rich and connected," Shannon stated.

"What will you do now?" Rex switched the brolly to his other arm to relieve his aching muscles. He had hoped for some mellow May sunshine for his trip south.

"Now I'll have to hire a new designer." Shannon chewed on her lip, looking in that moment more like a schoolgirl than a London sophisticate. "Look, I have to go, but you can come by my office anytime." She pulled a business card from her black suede handbag, declining his offer to escort her to her car.

Rex watched as her high heels propelled her

around puddles to the zippy Fiat 500 Cabrio parked at the curb. Not exactly a sports car, as defined by the nightclub witness, but silver grey nonetheless. And how reliable had his account been, after all? Presumably he'd had a few drinks that night.

Rex decided to dig around some more, proceeding with the chauffeur.

Erik Christiansen was waiting by the silver stretch limo, taut as steel and professionally impervious to the rain, his black cap dripping onto the darkening shoulders of his black uniform. Rex approached, anticipating a frosty reception, and was not disabused. Christiansen claimed to know nothing about the hit-and- run and little about the personal affairs of the family. He merely drove the various members about town and occasionally into neighbouring counties to visit friends at their country estates. Unlike the melodious intonations of Gino Giannelli, he spoke flawless, almost unaccented English, interspersed with the occasional Americanism. An experienced Crown prosecutor, Rex felt certain Christiansen knew more than he was telling. The words sounded rehearsed, the pale eyes veered from his own or else held them too long. At that moment, Sir Howes appeared at the gate with his wife, his remaining daughter, and the relic aunts. Christiansen took off toward them with a golf umbrella, leaving Rex to plan his next move. Lunch.

~ * ~

Presto's proved to be more illuminating this time around, once Rex circumvented the tight-lipped wait staff and convinced the behind-the-scenes employees he was not from the police. He discovered that the head chef, when adequately compensated for the information, had a cousin who was a house agent, and said cousin had sublet a body repair shop to "GiGi," as Gino Giannelli was affectionately known at the bistro. Most of the employees were from the same region in Southern Italy as GiGi, if not the same town, and "took care" of their own. Yet they would sell their grandmother for a big enough bribe, Rex ruminated as he left the premises with a considerably lighter wallet—and the name of the property agent in Soho.

Next, he made his way to Elise's home on foot and arrived at a late Georgian building split into ten flats and serviced by a porter wearing a waistcoat. Doubtless apprised by Sir Howes or Mr. Whitmore of Rex's business, the elderly man let him into number five without a murmur of protest. Here Rex found Jennifer dressed in slacks and a puce angora sweater sifting through a morass of papers and photos in the front drawing room. Joining her on the white leather sectional, Rex told her his business and apologized for the imposition.

"You're the Scottish barrister who solved the

murders at Swanmere Manor."

"Among others."

"And you're hoping to find the hit-and-run driver?"

"If at all possible."

"Could be anyone. London is a big place."

"Well, I know *that*. But your father feels it was closer to home, so to speak. Call it paternal instinct." Or paranoia.

Jennifer drew her inelegant legs beneath her chin. Her bare feet were bereft of nail varnish, just as her face was nude of visible makeup. Rex reflected once more on the vagaries of genetics. And yet her equine features were not unattractive in a singularly British way.

"Looking for anything in particular?" he asked, cocking his head at the pile of papers between them on the plush sofa.

"Just private stuff my sister wouldn't have wanted anybody to see. I just want to protect her."

"You two were close?"

"Oh, yes. We never had any secrets."

However, Jennifer admitted to having no clue as to why Elise had gone to Presto's unless it was to meet Gino. The phone conversation with her sister on Friday afternoon had concerned a family brunch the next day at Claridge's, a monthly event organized by the decrepit aunts, and which the girls attended in hopes of a sizeable inheritance, being the sole viable heirs.

"Do you have a job, Miss Howes?" Rex asked.

She regarded him blankly. "I have my allowance and still live at home, but I'm staying here for a few days to sort out Elise's things. I do a lot of charity work, of course. Mummy's very much into that sort of thing. It's the duty of the privileged class, she says, and of a politician's wife. And why take a job away from someone who actually needs it? Elise only got into business because she couldn't find any hats she really liked. She always was rather artistic. I'm the practical one."

Rex smiled in spite of himself. He felt he might get somewhere with Jennifer Howes. She came across as earnest and eager to please. "I gather Shannon Smythe is the practical one in your sister's enterprise."

"I suppose so. Elise could never have managed without her. No head for figures *at all!*"

"And Shannon has, I take it."

"Oh, yes. She helped sort out Gino's taxes, which were a dreadful mess."

"I thought Shannon didn't like Elise's fiancé." Rex saw no reason not to stir the pot a little. Ms. Smythe had made it clear the two women did not care for each other.

Jennifer smirked. "Shows how little *you* know. I saw a bouquet of red roses on her desk. Two dozen." She paused for dramatic effect. "They were from him."

"From Gino?" The girl nodded. "Was there a card?" he asked.

"Yes, and it said, *'Your devoted Gino.'* I just happened to notice." The young woman had the decency to blush.

"Did Elise know about this?"

"Unlikely. She was out of town that week."

"Ah."

The roses struck a discordant note in his mind. Had Shannon lied to him about her feelings for Gino? Most women, in his prosaic experience, while perhaps loath to consign a lavish bouquet of roses to the bin, would nonetheless discard the note of an unwelcome admirer. And if Shannon liked him so little, why had she helped with his finances? As a favour to Elise? Very puzzling, he thought. One thing to ponder, however: Gino could be a man who said it— whatever the occasion—with flowers.

"Did he ever give you flowers?"

Jennifer's hand went to her throat and fingered a string of pearls. "Me? Why?"

"I heard he received a loan from your sister for his luxury car venture. Thanks in part to you."

"That's right. She wrote out a cheque to him for fifty thousand pounds."

"When was this exactly?"

"This past Friday, according to this counterfoil." She showed it to Rex.

"Funny. I spoke to Gino and he said he hadn't seen Elise since Sunday of the week before."

26

"He might have picked it up from the receptionist. Elise had a hair appointment Friday afternoon, so he might have missed her."

"Aye, perhaps. One more thing, Miss Howes. Do you drive?"

"Yes, sort of. I mean, I have my learner's permit."

After thanking Jennifer for her cooperation, Rex took his leave with parting words of solace, though he knew from experience how inadequate such words could be, having lost his wife to breast cancer when his son was fifteen.

He decided, in light of Jennifer's revelation, to take up Ms. Smythe's invitation. Thanking a woman with a large bouquet of red roses for helping with one's taxes seemed to Rex an extravagant, even romantic, gesture. Retrieving the business card Shannon had given him, he arranged to meet with the *modiste* at her office suite, located in Park Lane close to where he was staying.

A cheery yellow sofa welcomed visitors to the second-floor lobby of Head Start!, where a collection of headpieces displayed on tall stands provided further flourishes of colour and texture, and offset the concept of works of art in themselves. Several were adorned with exotic feathery plumes, realistic peppermint candy canes, and glass cocktail twizzlers, frivolous affairs in Rex's opinion. He reflected it would take a very confident woman to wear some of these fantastical creations perched on her person, although they might look not out of place on a Milan or Paris runway. As he examined them, he looked for price tags, curious as to what the cost of high fashion might be…

"Mr. Graves?" enquired a skirt-suited young woman stepping into the room. "Shannon will see you now."

Pivoting in the direction whence she had come, she led the way to her employer's office. Declining Ms. Smythe's offer of a cappuccino, Rex settled into one of two comfortable bucket armchairs across from her desk and came straight to the point.

"Miss Smythe, may I ask—do you have a special young man in your life?"

The fulsome young woman, who had changed out of mourning, blushed beneath her crimson beret. "I don't." She laughed unconvincingly. "Where would I find the time?"

"Cards on the table, Miss Smythe. Gino declared his devotion to you with roses, did he not?"

Shannon blushed more alarmingly now, almost matching the hue of her felt cap. "That's only because I helped him with his taxes."

"If I may be so bold, you remind me of a young Sophia Loren, and I'm sure your charms are not lost on a hot-blooded Italian."

"Wow. You're not one to beat about the bush!" Shannon chewed on her fingernail while

Rex waited patiently for an admission he was sure was forthcoming. She struck him as basically a straightforward young woman. "Oh, why am I protecting the wanker?" she said at length. Sitting back in her executive chair, she took a shuddering breath. "Yes, I was having a sordid fling with Gino. And you cannot imagine the guilt I feel, especially now, with Elise dead. Some friend I turned out to be," she added.

"You were with him Friday night?"

"I was. And yes, I lied to the police about staying home giving myself a pedicure. I knew he was meeting Elise for a late dinner, but we got carried away."

"He finally went off to meet her? On foot?"

Shannon nodded and looked at him full-on across the desk. "And I'll tell you this much. I saw him pocket a container of pills as he was getting dressed. A full container, mind. When I asked what they were for, he said they were aspirin for his headache. He had certainly not been complaining of a headache just minutes before."

"What do you think the pills were?"

"XTC, I'm sure of it. He'd tried to get me to take it once at a party, and I recognized the bottle, which is a regular aspirin bottle. He'd got Elise hooked. I could tell he was lying about a headache, but it was like he didn't care if I knew he was lying or not."

Rex asked himself whether drugs had been found in Elise's system, and, if so, that fact had been hushed up. Dick Whitmore had only told him about her alcohol intake. "You think he planned to drug Elise?" he asked. "Why?"

Shannon swivelled this way and that in her chair. "She intended to cancel the cheque for the loan. I think that snitch of a sister told her about the roses Gino sent me."

Perhaps this information had been imparted during the Friday afternoon phone conversation with Jennifer. Being stood up at the bistro was probably the clincher for Elise, and she had confronted her fiancé. That same night she was killed in a hit-and-run just steps from her home. Mere coincidence?

"Did you tell him Elise was going to cancel the fifty thousand pounds?"

"He already knew. I wouldn't have told him, in any case. He has a filthy temper."

"Then you most definitely should stay away from him," Rex said in a fatherly tone.

"I know. I don't even like him. He's just so bloody hard to resist."

"Resist," he told her in no uncertain terms, warming his words with a smile.

Eyes downcast, Shannon murmured resolutely that she would.

Now, Rex thought; who had told Gino about Elise's decision to cancel the cheque? Three guesses it was Jennifer, trying again to get on his good side—if, in fact, he had one. After some delay getting her phone number, and a good deal of prevaricating on her part, he was able to ascertain that she had indeed warned Gino and had told Elise about the roses. He deduced this last act had been out of jealousy and spite.

Postponing his dinner plans, Rex made for Sloane Car Service to pursue his conversation with Erik Christiansen, which had been curtailed that morning at the cemetery. After the interview he would head back to Wellington House and see what Mr. Whitmore's housekeeper had prepared for his dinner. His last meal, a savoury steak and kidney pie coiffed in flaky pastry, had been accompanied by a bottle of rather good claret. Ignoring the rumblings in his stomach, he pursued his destination. Business before pleasure, he reminded himself, especially when the business was murder.

~ * ~

He found Erik Christiansen in a subterranean garage lined with luxury sedans polishing the chrome on the silver limo. Dressed in black livery, he straightened when he saw Rex. He was about two inches shy of the older man's six-four without his cap, which hung from the hood ornament.

"Tell me what you know," Rex urged the Howes' family chauffeur, sensing that a direct plea would elicit more confidence than a bribe. "I sense there's something more than you let on earlier."

"I really don't know anything. And I don't want to lose my best client."

"Sir Howes is the one who retained my services, so we're working for the same person. Anything you can tell me that relates to his dead daughter, however insignificant it may have appeared to you at the time, would be appreciated. And, hopefully, helpful in finding the driver who knocked her down."

With a brief look around the garage, Christiansen nodded. "But just so you understand, this is a good gig and I don't want to lose it."

"Understood."

"So, Friday night, I dropped her parents off at a dinner in Mayfair and was cruising around looking for a place to eat, when I saw her leave Presto's. I stopped the car and she got in. She said she'd been stood up."

"By Gino?"

"Yeah. She was close to tears, but more angry, you know? I tried to comfort her."

"And how did you do that?" The icy Christiansen did not strike Rex as the hugging, soothing type.

"I kissed her. She kissed me back. She was tipsy, that's for sure. We kissed for a while. It seemed to make her feel better. Don't tell Sir Howes any of this. She told me she was going to break off the engagement with Gino. Pride had prevented her from calling him to find out where he was, and sometimes he didn't answer her calls. I thought this strange. Gino was on to a good thing. Why screw up? Elise was rich and beautiful, with a powerful father. Anyway, she finally told me to let her out of the car. She wanted to walk home."

"Did she walk in that direction, or in the opposite direction towards Gino's place?"

"Towards her place. I insisted she let me drive her. Her father would have wanted me to. I mean, she was in no state…but she said the air would do her good."

"She had no flowers with her at that point?"

"Flowers? No. Just a handbag."

"Mr. Christiansen, how long have you been driving the Howes?"

"Eight, nine months."

"Have you been in London long?"

"Long enough to know my way around."

"Essential in your line of work, I imagine. Is this your only line of work?"

Christiansen flushed pink beneath his pale skin. "I'm training for the stage. I lived in L.A. for a time doing the valet-acting thing, but I thought I might get further if I came here to study as a Shakespearean actor. I hope to get into the RSC and perhaps go back to the States later."

Rex wished him good luck and said he'd make a good Hamlet. The Dane gave the faintest of smiles and got back to his task of sprucing up the limo.

"By the way, do you know where the Italian Ambassador lives?" Rex asked over his shoulder. "It would save me time looking it up."

Christiansen straightened his lean frame, the polishing cloth dangling from his right hand. "Of course. He's a friend of Sir Howes. He was the guest of honour at the club party that night." He gave Rex the address.

~ * ~

Rex waited in line at the coffee house across the street from his borrowed flat. Done out in shades of brown and beige, with a framed floor-to-ceiling mirror behind the polished wood counter, the café exuded a fragrance of French custard and the aroma of freshly ground coffee beans. He ordered a latte and two pastries, and took his breakfast into the park.

A solitary green bench in a corner beckoned among the copper beech, oak, and horse chestnut trees. He sat enjoying the watery sunshine, while drifts of creamy white blossoms ruffled in the breeze at his feet, and savoured the moment along with his breakfast before making his first in-person call of the day.

The previous night after dinner he had spread his notes across the living room table and moved the angle poise lamp from the small desk. He had worked for a while in the pool of light, making annotations and studying photos of the scene of the accident. Then, chewing on his dry pipe as he contemplated the framed posters on the wall depicting red maple leaves in autumnal Beijing, he had considered likely scenarios relating to the hit-and-run, based on the facts supplied by Mr. Whitmore and on his own information. One stood out. Abruptly he had left his work on the table and gone out on a clandestine mission.

He now watched in distraction while a dishevelled old woman, the front buttons on her tweed coat misaligned, rolled a shopping bag made of stiff tartan cloth along the diagonal path through the park. The material bulged with elongated cylindrical shapes. Rex was in no doubt as to what the zipped-up bag contained. Whatever the lady's alcoholic preference, she appeared eager to get home to consume it and proceeded at a purposeful clip. Would Elise Howes, with her predilection for drink, have ended up the same way? he wondered.

A sudden gust ripped through the trees sending a new shower of woodsy- scented chestnut blooms onto the grass. Retrieving his black brolly, he rose from the bench. He discarded the coffee container and pastry box in a corrugated iron bin, and exited the park. On the street he hailed a black cab, giving the driver the Italian Ambassador's address.

Vittorio Scalfaro was home, confined to a day bed in the drawing room with a professed migraine, and draped in a silk robe of midnight blue. He was almost comically flabbergasted when the Scotsman told him he had found his silver Ferrari in Giannelli's "other" garage undergoing a touch-up.

"You found my stolen car?"

Judging by the decor, the ambassador was a man of refined taste, and Rex felt frumpy by comparison. But Scalfaro was not a good liar, at least not for a diplomat.

"Not stolen, Ambassador," Rex said pointedly. "Merely temporarily out of commission. Your private club gave me a list of the valet-parked cars for Friday night. Yours was returned to you without a scratch shortly before Miss Howes' accident."

The man's clean-shaven face sank into blurred lines. Rex decided to cut him some slack. Scalfaro appeared to be suffering enough.

"You probably did not see the young woman step out onto the street. A van blocked your visibility, and it was dark. Had the wheel been on the right-hand side, you might have seen her sooner and had a chance to break."

"Alas, so true!" The ambassador spoke in melodious tones, like Gino's. "I should have bought a car with British steering, but I planned on driving the Ferrari back to Italy. Signorina Howes leapt out of nowhere! I felt the impact and took off in a blind panic. I didn't realize at the time that the pedestrian was Sir Howes' daughter. I thought I should get home right away and seek legal advice. After all, a person in my position… How would it look?"

"Worse now," Rex informed him. "The police will suspect you of drinking. And charge you with fleeing the scene of an accident."

Scalfaro raised his hands in supplication. "A gin and tonic and two glasses of wine with dinner. It is conceivable I was going too fast— one always does in Ferraris, but traffic was light. I am filled with remorse. But, what can be proved?"

Not a lot, Rex thought; except that the man was a coward. To top it all, he had diplomatic immunity from prosecution. What, he enquired out of interest, had Scalfaro's legal advice been?

"To wait on events. When no one was able to identify my car, my attorney suggested I get it fixed without delay using the utmost discretion. The repercussions as Italian Ambassador to the UK could be embarrassing in the extreme, and Parliament has enough embarrassment to deal with. If only I could turn back the clock of that terrible night!" Scalfaro lamented.

Aye, thought Rex, but the girl would probably be dead anyhow, at Giannelli's hands.

And what did Rex plan to do with this information? the ambassador asked, rising shakily from the Victorian day bed.

"Not my decision," Rex told him, excusing himself with a curt goodbye.

It was time to confront Gino Giannelli.

~ * ~

Rex consulted his notebook for the business address Mr. Whitmore had provided, and availed himself of the waiting cab. A shower broke out as they took off down the quiet leafy street and turned onto a thoroughfare. Rex sat back on the worn seat and re-ordered his thoughts. Getting some sort of confession or at least confirmation of his hypothesis from Elise's fiancé would be crucial to wrapping up the case.

"But the police searched my premises." The young Italian spread his arms wide, indicating the breadth of hangar filled with a half dozen imported luxury cars. He gestured impatiently to a mechanic to leave them. The place was immaculate, the smell of new tires and engine oil intoxicating. Rex who, incongruously for his size, drove an economical Mini Cooper, found himself seduced by the sleek long bonnets and sexy rear ends of these gas-hungry predators. Gino caressed the moulded front quarter panel of a cherry red Maserati GranTurismo with almost sensual pleasure. Clearly these machines were his passion.

"I was referring to a body shop which you omitted to tell the detectives aboot," Rex enlightened him. "I saw a freshly sprayed silver Ferrari in there." He had shinnied up a drainpipe the previous night with a pocket torch, a precarious endeavour considering his bulk, but in the pursuit of justice worth the risk of a broken ankle.

"So?"

"It made me curious and more than a little suspicious, especially when I saw the diplomatic plate. I traced it back to a Vittorio Scalfaro whom you sold it to in March. Your personal assistant was very helpful when I called this morning posing as a potential buyer. As was the house agent who found you the new premises." And Mr. Whitmore, of course. The solicitor had identified the Ferrari as belonging to the Italian Ambassador, a friend of Sir Howes'.

"Your point?" Gino demanded, showing impatience.

"The ambassador came to you for a repair job—a little *quid pro quo*."

"What do you mean?"

"He'd been dining in Mayfair and left the club shortly before the accident, in which he has admitted his involvement. Perhaps he saw you at the scene."

"He didn't. Nobody saw me." Gino fell silent, realizing his error. His hand struck the two-door coupé he'd been fondling. "*Merda!*" he swore.

"Say It with Flowers stays open late at the weekend. The girl at the shop told me a man fitting your description paid cash for a bunch of chrysanthemums just before closing. Mums?" Rex asked emphatically, raising an eyebrow.

"They were a peace offering for being late," Gino explained—warily.

"Roses are more romantic, not so?"

"The roses were drooping and sad. I liked the look of the golden balls. So sunny, so alive! I got them on the way to her place."

"Spur of the moment?"

"That is how I am. Impulsive. They told me at Presto's she had left not long before. I saw her on the street and called out her name."

"What then?"

"I explained I had overslept from a nap and was coming over to her flat to surprise her. I offered to walk her home, but she was having none of it. She was angry, and a little drunk. She only accepted the flowers when I threatened to throw them in the gutter. The next thing that happened was an accident. She stepped into the road still shouting at me over her shoulder. The driver took off in a hurry, and I couldn't make out the number plate. It happened so fast."

Giannelli mopped his brow with the cuff of his spotless blue overalls. "I knew Elise's father would blame me, even though it wasn't my fault, so I left when I saw another person coming to her aid." Rex felt sure he would have fled anyway. "Later, when Vittorio dropped off his Ferrari, I had my suspicions. A yellow petal was stuck in the grille."

"But you couldn't be sure he hadn't seen you, so you did the repair, no questions asked."

Giannelli made no reply.

"The good Samaritan heard Elise say 'Chris' and 'Jean' with her dying breath. I suspect she was trying to say "chrysanthemums" and managed the first part of your name, Gin-o. The chrysanthemum in your country represents death. The flowers you gave her were a death warning. Not true?" A sous-chef at Presto's had supplied this interesting titbit when Rex asked if chrysanthemums were popular in Italy, thus confirming what his suicidal ex-girlfriend had told him.

Gino shook his head derisively, going so far as to tap his temple to indicate the Scotsman's lack of sanity. "You are reading too much into all of this."

Undeterred, Rex continued his theory. "You heard the powerful engine of a speeding car and pushed Elise in front of it, not realizing it was Scalfaro's Ferrari. The left-hand drive may have afforded the ambassador less reaction time as Elise 'leapt' onto the street, as he described it. A wee push by you in her inebriated state would have sufficed."

"*Vaffanculo!*" Dark fire flashed in Gino's eyes. While Rex did not understand what had just been said, it sounded obscene nonetheless. "Why would I want to kill her?"

"Several reasons. First, you saw her in the limo with Christiansen and got jealous."

"I admit I saw her with the chauffeur, but she

got out soon afterwards, and I followed."

"Even though you were cheating on Elise, you didn't like seeing her kiss another man. But you had planned to kill her anyway, before she could cancel the cheque for your business. Hence the Ecstasy, which Shannon saw you take with you and which you would have rammed down Elise's throat once you got her home, and then made it look like suicide. But she blew you off on the street, and her indiscretion with the Dane served to add fuel to the fire. You saw another opportunity for murder when that Ferrari came tearing down the road. Impulsive and spur of the moment," Rex added with a mirthless smile. "Is that not how you described yourself?"

"You can't prove any of this!" Giannelli said, echoing his compatriot.

Maybe not, Rex thought grimly. It was all circumstantial, but the accusations had certainly got the wind up the hot-headed Italian. And he wouldn't be giving Shannon any more roses.

Rex called the solicitor upon leaving Gino's garage and made an appointment to report his findings.

"Premeditated murder is not easy to prove in this case," Rex concluded at Mr. Whitmore's office. The solicitor sitting at his desk was a fussy little man with womanish hands. "Giannelli caught a lucky break if his intention was to O.D.

his fiancée. A reckless driver beat him to the punch, with perhaps a little help from Casanova. Elise Howes was drunk and probably distracted to-boot, so it was a perfect opportunity. Pure coincidence it was one of Giannelli's cars."

"Ye-es," Mr. Whitmore said ruminatively. The tapered fingers, on which glinted a bejewelled wedding ring, drummed the mahogany surface of the antique partners' desk. "Well, we had better just stick to the facts. Sir Howes can draw his own conclusions. It won't be the news he anticipated, of course. What a devastating thing to have happen. Vittorio Scalfaro's reputation will be ruined if this gets out. However, that Sir Howes' prospective son-in-law was cheating on his daughter will come as no surprise. But I would have credited Shannon with more sense." The solicitor checked his gold Rolex and grabbed a hat and umbrella from the coat tree behind his door. "Sir Howes is expecting us. There's a car waiting outside."

The cabinet minister resided at Wilton Crescent in a grand terrace house five stories high, a frill of black iron balconies adorning the stone clad façade. He received his guests once again in the rich wood-panelled library and offered them sherry, barely able to disguise his displeasure when he heard the results of Rex's investigation. It soon became clear he intended to make public Vittorio Scalfaro's involvement in his daughter's death.

"What a can of worms," he growled, turning to Rex. "And Giannelli sold him that Ferrari. Bloody stupid, if you ask me, bombing around in one of those dangerous toys. And then my future son-in-law left my little girl to die on the street. He might've well have just killed her himself."

Rex privately concurred.

~ * ~

Several weeks later at his chambers in Edinburgh, Rex received a call from Mr. Whitmore to the effect that Gino Giannelli had overdosed on Ecstasy. He had been found by his cleaning lady drowned in his bathtub, naked among a sprinkling of floating petals. A card in Italian found on the tile floor, and subsequently leaked to the press, thanked Gino for making the sender's time in London more pleasurable; however, in view of Gino's past connection with the Howes family and the "unfortunate accident," the flowers were being sent not only as a token of tender affection but of regretful adieu. Signed, "Vitto."

There existed no possibility in Rex's mind that a lovelorn Gino had committed suicide, still less that he was homosexual, as the message and flowers insinuated. The Italian Ambassador had vehemently denied sending either, as, in the mind of the public, he would. Rex could not suppress a wry smile of appreciation at the apt and subtle revenge exacted on Gino and Vittorio Scalfaro.

"A curiously Shakespearean concept," he remarked to Mr. Whitmore, reflecting on the watery grave and ironic floral touch.

"Quite," replied the Howes family solicitor, adding that his client had made it quite clear that he did not require Rex's assistance in this particular case.

"Mum's the word," the Scotsman acknowledged, appropriately, he thought.

However, as a man of the law, he felt somewhat conflicted.

Apparently Sir Howes, with the aid of his loyal Danish factotum, had prescribed justice to his full satisfaction.

THE END

ABOUT THE AUTHOR

C.S. Challinor was raised and educated in Scotland (St. George's School for Girls, Edinburgh) and England (Lewes Priory, Sussex; University of Kent, Canterbury: Joint Hons Latin & French). She also holds a diploma in Russian from the Pushkin Institute in Moscow. She now lives in Southwest Florida. Challinor is a member of the Authors Guild and writes the critically acclaimed Rex Graves cozy mystery series published by Midnight Ink, featuring Rex Graves, a Scottish barrister and amateur sleuth.

Christmas Is Murder, the first in the Rex Graves Mystery series, reached #1 on the Kindle Bestseller List. This title is also available in Large Print hardcover through Thorndike Reviewer's Choice. The fifth in the series, *Murder of the Bride*, was a Mystery Guild Book Club pick (hardcover) and a Top Five Books of 2011 Selection by *Crime Fiction Lover*. The latest novel in the series, *Upstaged by Murder*, has just been released in all formats, including Large Print.

Visit the author at www.rexgraves.com.

50158105R00027

Made in the USA
Middletown, DE
23 June 2019